EVERY-THING

ALL AT ONCE

EVERY-THING THING ALL AT ONCE

STEVEN CAMDEN

AKA POLARBEAR

CAMDEN

MACMILLAN CHILDREN'S BOOKS

For you,
holding this book in your hand right now
You are brave and you are brilliant
Remember that always

First published 2018 by Macmillan Children's Books
an imprint of Pan Macmillan
20 New Wharf Road, London N1 9RR
Associated companies throughout the world
www.panmacmillan.com

ISBN 978-1-5098-8003-4

CONTENTS

PROLOGUE

What's it about then?

Well,

It's about the tapestry of moments, woven of a thousand threads.

Different versions of the world swirling inside a thousand heads.

We go from the biggest to the smallest, dropped off, left to fend,

in the secondary school jungle jumbled enemies, new friends.

It's a war zone. It's a haven. It's a stage full of bright lights.

It's a series of scary alleyways walked on a dark night.

Always moving. Unforgiving.

Full of music. Full of living.

Zoom in. One mind. Split screen. Another mind. Another mind.

Another mind. Another mind.

And another mind.

All together. Same place.

Same walls. Same space.

Every emotion under the sun. Faith lost. Victories won.

It doesn't stop.

Until the bell. Now it's heaven. Now it's hell.

Who knows? Not me.

I just wrote what I can see.

So what's it about?

Here's my response:

It's about Everything, All At Once.

EVERY EMOTION UNDER
THE SUN. FAITH LOST.
VICTORIES WON.

IT DOESN'T STOP.

UNTIL THE BELL. NOW
IT'S HEAVEN. NOW
IT'S HELL.

WHO KNOWS? NOT ME.

FIRST DAY

It looks like a spaceship
a jagged silver spaceship
windows like portals
reflecting the light
no
it looks like the head of
a massive metal monster
its sliding glass mouth
with teeth ready to bite
no
it looks like it sprouted right
out of the floor
ripped through rock, dirt and gravel
burst out of the ground
no
it looks like it fell
from some alien planet
crash-landed on earth
with some terrible sound
no
it looks like
it looks like
I don't know what it looks like
Massive and scary

Noisy
Alive
I feel like a mouse
stepping into the jungle
Tell my mum that I love her
I'm going inside.

MORNING STATE

Through the gates
past the bikes
wave to Tanya
dodge a fight

Text to Mum
Arrived. I'm safe
switch it off
they confiscate

Cut past science
slip inside
wave of students
catch a ride

Reach the toilets
fix my face
check my homework
pencil case

Meet Sabrina
by the hall
Were you on Facebook?
You see his wall?

Walk together
through the rush
spot Jerome
secret crush

Mr Thomas
warden stare
too much stomach
not much hair

Outside form room
join the line
Zak and Sean are trying to rhyme

Michaela's shouting
something mean
Theresa's crying
drama queen

It's just the standard
morning state

another Monday
in Year 8.

WHAT?

HER AND THINGY?

HER AND WHO?

AT THE PARTY

WHAT PARTY?

Did you hear about Lisa?

What? Why you whispering?

Lisa

Which Lisa?

Lisa Lisa

My Lisa?

No

Year 10 Lisa?

Is Lisa in Year 10?

Year 10 Lisa is

OK, yeah

Year 10 Lisa?

Yeah

What about her?

You didn't hear?

Hear what?

Oh, man

What?

Her and thingy?

Her and who?

At the party

What party?

On Saturday. Liam's party.

You were there?

Nah, I had to go to my cousin's, but I heard

Heard what?

Her and thingy

Thingy who?

Oh, my days

Tell me!

Shhh! I'll tell you later. She's looking.

No she isn't

Yes she is

Tell me now

Sorry, Miss. Nothing. Just about the work. Sorry.

Yes, Miss, about the work. Sorry.

We will, Miss. Yeah.

Yes, Miss. Course. Sorry.

OUTSIDE FRENCH

I'm a dot
in one of those pictures   made up of dots

the ones
where you zoom out and see

the face of Yoda

Only in this one   when you zoom out

you just see me

much older.

DOUBLE AGENT

Je m'appelle Yusef
J'ai quatorze ans
J'aime jouer au football et lire des bandes dessinées
J'ai deux frères plus âgés
Je fais semblant que je ne suis pas bon en français
Mais,
Ma mère vient de Toulouse
Nous parlons seulement français à la maison
Donc ça a toujours l'impression de tricher

Pardon.

Sorry.

So it always feels like cheating
We only speak French at home
My mum is from Toulouse
But,
I pretend I'm not good at French
I have two older brothers
I like playing football and reading comics
I'm fourteen
My name is Yusef

YOU'RE STARING. STOP STARING.

I'M TRYING TO

HELP YOU, IF THEY SEE YOU

STARE

YOU'RE A GONER.

ANYONE

Everyone's writing
except me
blank page
staring back
like it's laughing
saying,
What's wrong with you?
What is wrong with me?
Why don't you get it?
Why don't I get it?
Are you stupid?
Am I stupid?
Why are you just sitting here, frozen?
I don't know
What is this feeling?
Feels like pain
like actual pain
like it hurts
to not know
what everyone else does
how come it's only me
who seems to be
lost?

MICHAEL VS HIS BRAIN (AGAIN)

Don't stare.
Don't stare.
Why you staring for?

I'm not.
I'm not.
I don't wanna.

You're staring. Stop staring.
I'm trying to
help you, if they see you
stare
you're a goner.

So don't let me stare, think
of
something else

It's not me.

It is you.
You're doing it

I am not.

It's you.

What am I meant to do?

Just do something that's not
gonna
      ruin it.

Why you singing?   Stop singing

Who's singing?

You're singing! You can't sing
      you'll give
            us away

But you love singing.

No I don't!

Yes you do.

So what!
That's still no   reason
        to say.

Now what are you doing?

Nothing

You're dancing

I'm not

Yes you are!   You're really   not   getting it.
        You can't dance

I can dance

I know, but not   here   you dance and I end
        up
                regretting it

So what can I do?

Nothing.

You can do nothing.　　Just sit here

　　and don't

　　　　make a sound

　　　　Just let me blend in

　　　　　　You don't wanna blend in

　　　　　　I know,　　　　but I have to

　　　　　　　for

　　　　　　　now.

VENDING MACHINE

I can't believe her
and Carly won't say, but I know she can't either.
I had to get away from them to try and get a breather
cos I swear I could feel my blood running up a fever

I can't tell if it's real, or some nightmarish dream
as I walk to the lower school vending machine

She knew I liked him.
I told her back on the end of Year 9 trip.
Four nights in Ireland, sharing a room,
her saying she thought it was best to stay silent,
You shouldn't let him know yet, you need to be sure
Let me speak to my brother, they've been friends since Year 4.

What a snake.
She tricked me and made her own plan.
I take out my money to pay for my can.
The nerve of her.
I bet he'd never even heard of her. Now she's happily stepped in to
    steal my life
like a murderer.

Money in. Button pushed.
Heavy heart. Stomach crushed.

I should slap her.

Yeah right. Like that's gonna happen.
There's a bunch of Year 8s by the cloak room all rapping
badly
bobbing and waving hands madly and the one on the end
yeah, he's staring
right at me. Like,
right at me.

And it's like his eyes shoot out this small bolt of happy.
Bless him.
My heavy heart is telling me that I should send a message
to let him know I've noticed and that the feeling is a present.
His friends don't even clock it how he's not inside their bubble
and he has no idea how much that look can lead to trouble.
Trust me, little man,
You leave yourself exposed when your heart is there to see
and some evil feet will trample on the part that makes you free
but I promise you, it's worth it
the magic
the frozen space and time
sometimes it leaves you powerless, but now the power's mine.

So I smile
Right at him. Like,
right at him
see it land
the bell goes
he understands

It's possible
you never know, stay ready, be a fighter
Then
I take my can and walk away
my heart a little lighter.

Yo, you hear about David?

Which David?

What you mean, which David? David

With the ponytail?

Nah, with the hi-top

Hi-Top David?

Yes

What happened?

You didn't hear?

Hear what?

Him and thingy

Thingy who?

Exactly. Right?

What?

At the party

Which party?

On Saturday. Liam's party. You should've been there, fam

You went?

Nah, I just heard

Heard what?

About David, are you listening?

You didn't say anything

I'm trying to tell you. David.

Hi-Top David.

Yo, can I speak?

Yeah

Bum, so David, yeah?

Yeah?

And thingy, at Liam's party, on Saturday, one sec. Yo, Marlon!
How you gonna miss from there,

man? You see that?

Tell me about David

Oh yeah, yeah, so David, yeah?

Yeah.

Oh yo, that's the bell. I got History. I can't be late again, trust
me, Mr Bailey is gunning for man

Hold up, what about David? And thingy? At the party?

Relax, fam. I'll tell you at lunch.

SHAUNA SAID THAT

LEIA SAID THAT

JORDAN SAID IT'S OVER

IT'S COMPLICATED

Shauna said that

    Leia said that

        Jordan said it's over

He changed his status yesterday

before he even told her

And now although I'm Leia's friend   and should offer my shoulder

I'm kinda hoping Jordan will be mine

        like he's supposed to.

SCIENCE BLOCK TOILETS

The drip of the tap like
the tick of a clock
as I sit on the top of the seat gripping the lock
It's break-time and I'm hiding
not from anyone
really
I just wanted some time without anyone near me
to breathe
in the midst of the chaos and noise
hyena girls and megaphone boys
police captain mannequin teachers
a gaggle of mad daggering laminate features
leeches attach on to top of the pack creatures
between bells they speak spells to keep sweet the divas
a legion of chair feet screeches
and I feel the bones in my ears crack
the CD skips
between these lips, my tongue whispers
You won't ever get these years back.
So I'm here
to sit
while the crowds are outside
in my graffitied bubble
I pause and unwind.

And I read lines, scribbled and scratched into patterns
declarations of feelings
bad stuff that's happened

Sophie loves Toby 4 eva

NO, COS SOPHIE KISSED JONAH
ON THE COACH DOWN TO DEVON

No I never   Why you lying?

No she's not. I saw you. Slapper. Stop crying.

I HATE MATHS!

me too!

CARA G IS A BITCH

No she's not
YOU ARE
FOR SCRIBBLING THIS

The voices ring out
ricochet off the walls

and I'm trapped
in a casket of angry catcalls
my hand falls from the lock. I reach for my bag. The door starts to
creak. I smell bleach and I gag
and the voices are screeching
the volume has risen
my toilet seat haven   morphed into a prison

Then the bell goes
and no ring ever sounded so sweet
I pull open the door as I get to my feet
quick check in the mirror
Face is fine. All clear.
The tap drips approval and
the one voice I hear
is a small one
from a cubicle deep down
inside me
saying,
Next time you want peace
just go to the library.

EVERYTHING ELSE FEELS
LIKE SHOES

THAT DON'T FIT.

I CAN'T STARE AT A
COMPUTER

I CAN'T SCRIBBLE WHILE
I SIT

DEAR MUM, BTEC

I know you don't get it
the pleasure I feel
when I push down the pedal
the turn of the wheel

the buzz of the sander
the whirr of the drill
I breathe in the wood
my heart starts to fill

No words. No numbers.
No wasps in my brain
just the weight of the hammer
the bulb of the plane

my hands move
and things happen
I make grooves
and sing patterns

into pieces of trees
into plastic
and metal
feel the dust of the day
in my head start to settle

Sand. Repeat. Sand. Repeat.
Touch. Feel. Smooth. Complete.

It's a language that I speak
one that's disappearing
in the forest of the school
my favourite lesson is a clearing

Everything else feels like shoes
that don't fit.
I can't stare at a computer
I can't scribble while I sit

I have to be in it.
Touch it. Feel it
scratch my skin. Test my grip.
Show myself what real is.

Exams don't suit me.
I don't suit exams.
I understand the system
But, I'm drawing other plans

So don't worry when I tell you
that Uni's not the path I see
I'll build a future for myself, Mum,
and you'll be proud of me.

GOOD GIRL

Whatever teacher's teaching
whatever they're teaching
feeling pleased that their message is reaching me deeply
completing the puzzle and making
me smarter
charging me up to push and try harder

has no idea that
as I'm gazing out
my face is
the front
of an empty house.

AS I WATCH

At the back of Maths

while the rest of the class tackle graphs

Jack and Matt pass a note back and forth and cackle laughs.

Dominique is doing this thing with her feet, making both her heels
squeak on the leg of her seat

Morgan is awkwardly trying to yawn caught between feeling
naughty and boredom

Alissa and Kirstie sit earnestly working in search of a word of
approval from Sir

Gemma and Tristan pretend that they're listening nodding in sync
to prove that they've heard

Abdul is scribbling circles in curves filling his page with whirlpools
of o's

Dylan's pretending he's scratching his forehead secretly digging his
thumb up his nose

Famida's inspecting her nails like a surgeon

Arif is sneakily checking his phone

Dominic's holding his head like it's hurting

Abe is just slumped like a lump of old stone

and I sit, watching, drinking them in

making up rhymes for the lives that they live

cos that's my thing, sitting to the side, silently rhyming

capturing time with each blink of my eyelids

recording it all in a verse for just me

on my own in my head till the bell sets us free
and as we walk out I give my words marks out of ten
then head straight to next lesson where it all starts again.

FRAUD

If they found out
they'd move me away from my friends, slide me up with those kids
who sit smug at the front
the ones with rich parents and
monthly new trainers
whose lives feel like films
where they get what they want

My break-times would shatter into
shards of me lonely
cast off across bridges
I sent up in flames
the bonds that I've built
through shared
ghost dads and blankets
would snap as they all spat out
knives at my name

So I hide it.

Always.

Behind half-hearted nods

manufactured confusion

keep a grip on my hands

I let answers grow moss in the base of my skull

as I breathe in

the taste of

the fraud

that I am.

I DON'T KNOW WHAT YOU
CALL IT

I'VE NEVER FELT IT BEFORE

WHEN YOU FEEL LIKE YOU'RE
FLOATING

BUT STUCK TO THE FLOOR

IT HAPPENED THIS MORNING, NOW EVERYTHING'S CHANGED

So,

we were next to the cloakroom

five boys back again

same morning routine

every day at half ten

Jerome had his phone out

with Stormzy on loud

Zak was rhyming along to an invisible crowd

Sean was being his hype man

fingers stabbing the air

Malik was digging his afro comb

into his hair

I was sipping my grape juice

surveying the scene

then I saw her, right there

at the vending machine

And
WHAM!
Everything froze
Stormzy went silent
my friends struck a pose
It was like someone had pressed pause on the remote for the
    world
as I tilted my head
and stared at this girl

I don't know what you call it
I've never felt it before
when you feel like you're floating
but stuck to the floor
and I know it sounds cheesy
I know it's real lame
But the only thing I cared about
right then
was her name

'Who is she?'
I said
And the world kicked back in.
Zak and Sean with their concert
Malik's cheeky grin

'Who's who?' said Jerome
As he wheeled up the tune
'One more time!' shouted Zak,
'The bell's gonna go soon.'

'She's amazing,' I said,
quietly, under my breath
as I stared straight ahead
with my friends to my left.

She was stroking her lip
with her coin as she chose
and her uniform looked like
the most perfect clothes

She was older
no question
Year 11, or 10
light years out of my Year 8 league
but just then
she looked over
straight at me
and my body went numb
I felt like a planet
that orbits the sun

And right there
in that moment
nothing else mattered
I don't even care if you think
I'm being dramatic
I felt it
She felt it
the forces at play
Then the bell went
she smiled
and just walked away

It was perfect
and fleeting
a scene from a movie
I felt every emotion
go running right through me

'Yo, back here, lunchtime,'
said Zak
as they left.
I just nodded
still trying
to regain my breath.

MR BAILEY

There's that pause
a vacuum
slice
of a second
the minute hand quivers
before a new breath

They look up
like mice
silent timer conditioned
and when
the bell finally rings
they've already left

GAZELLE

Staring out of the window again
the green of the pitches is calling again
feel that itch in my muscles, the sigh in my bones
as the teacher's voice muffles, I drift on my own
breathe in, close my eyes
breathe out and I'm there
outside on the grass, surrounded by air
No talking, no questions, no turn of the screw
just the drum in my heart telling me what to do
so I
run
and I run
and I run and I run
and the faster I go
the more I become
I am bullet and arrow
and cheetah
gazelle
I am peregrine falcon and phoenix from hell
I am synapse and fibre and neuron
and flame
I am Thor's hammer lightning, too cosmic to tame
I am me
when I run

I can see

when I run

there is nothing that I cannot be when I run

I am anything

everything

cutting through time

And yet somehow

I'm completely

still in my mind

when I

run

can I

run

let me

run

long to

run

have to

run

and just

run

and just
run

and just

I MOVE WITH THE QUEUE
SLOWLY SHUFFLING MY FEET
MY HANDS GRIP MY TRAY
WAY TOO NERVOUS TO EAT

LUNCH LINE

I'm standing in line

behind people I don't know

queueing for food I don't like

Can somebody tell me

where do I go

to get a refund on my life?

THANKS A LOT, BELINDA

A thousand voices
fighting to speak
the scraping of plates
the squeaking of feet

The cackle of laughter
an embarrassed squeal
the packed lunchers trading
to get the best deal

I move with the queue
slowly shuffling my feet
my hands grip my tray
Way too nervous to eat

Eyes re-scan the room
sure to cover each zone
searching for someone
so I'm not alone

See,
that's the problem with best friends
no matter how cool:
who the hell do you sit with
when your best friend's off school?

FIGHT

There's fire in my blood
screams in my head
hands stabbing at my back
feet feel like lead

Tornado in my stomach
howling out for lunch
a pack of jeering, hungry dogs
begging me to punch

I look across into her eyes
confusion fighting terror
she's never known the random force
that's thrown us both together

But I have
I do
it's stitched into my body
the hard one, the scarred one
the one who's never sorry

That's who I am
I've always been
the character they made me
but something in this new girl's eyes
is saying it can save me

The crowd's howling, pushing, growling
teacher must be coming
they want to see my claws come out
before they all start running

But I can't move
I just stare
across into her eyes
and feel myself fill up with truth
that flushes out the lies

I don't want to be me
I want to be her
I don't want to be feared
I want to be heard

I'm tired of fighting
tired of frowning
tired of rolling my eyes
tired of drowning

I want to float
I want to talk
I want to hardly feel the ground beneath my feet
when I walk

I want to step into a room
and no one whispers or gets scared
I want to read a book
sit on the grass
and feel nobody care

We can help you
say her eyes
We can do that stuff together
we can disappear
into the crowd
and be ourselves
forever

Really?
Really.   *I hear you.*

She hears me.

So we do
this girl and me
we make a silent pledge
we leave our bodies
where they are and float
out to the edge

And as the crowd stands booing
the teacher cutting through
this girl and me
we walk away
off into something new.

STAFFROOM

It's that door
the unknown
teacher fortress
full blown
sorcery
secret powers
inside jokes
stolen hours

After bell
catch a glimpse
Mr Bailey, Mrs Simms
laughing?
What about?
Feeling queasy
full of doubt
don't trust it
or them
in there
together
why we not allowed inside
what they hiding, treasure?

It stinks
I say we storm it
an army full of uniform it's
doable
I know it
we have to overthrow it

who's with me?
raise a fist
weapons, smoke bombs
hazy mist

Anyone?
No?
Fine,
but don't bother coming crying.
These teachers keep the upper hand
cos none of us are trying.

NOTHING ELSE

Isn't that your little brother?

You can't choose
your family
but you can
hide
Turn just a fraction too slow
What? Where?
Let the ship of embarrassment
sail by
Somehow we share
genes
pieces of code that make me me
are in him too
so why is he like that?
He's always been different
Special, Mum said, but she never had to
watch friends stare, confused
while he sprints like a greyhound
in circles round the school
It makes him happy
like nothing else
Leave him to it
Suit yourself

Maybe he's part dog
simply happy with what he's got
You try and start a conversation and he's already gone
running
always running
but not away
more towards
running to something
I don't understand.

D4L (PART 3)
SCIENCE BLOCK TOILETS:
1.36 P.M.

Keep your voice down

Why?

It's delicate

What is? Why are we in here?

Cos it's quiet

What happened?

David and Lisa

What about them?

What do you think?

I have no idea

You don't?

No

No?

What? No. No way.

Yep.

For real?

That's what I heard

Shut up

Fine. Forget it then

David? And Lisa?

Yep. At Liam's party.

On Saturday?

Yeah

But I was there

So was I

I didn't see them. Hold up, who told you?

Does it matter?

Course it matters. Was it Reese?

Who cares?

I knew it. It's rubbish. Reese is full of it

No he isn't

Yes he is. Remember when he told everyone his dad was Kano's manager?

That was in Year 8

So what? He's still Reese

I guess

Allow him. Besides, Lisa don't even like David

How do you know?

Trust me. I can tell.

GOAL

It was perfect
the timing
like stars aligning or
looking up from your book when the class is silent
just as she does
so perfect you can feel it in your spine
the kind of moment that you know
will be engraved into your mind

Last minute
PE
Josh on the ball
I break free of my marker and give him the call
as I sprint into the box
Josh nutmegs his man
quick look up at me
I'm raising my hand
and he whips it
a perfect curve arcing my way
the keeper comes out
like he's certain to save
but I cut to the near post
spring
off my toes

sun cuts through the clouds like
the universe knows
this is meant to be
the perfect cross from Josh a gift
sent to me
my forehead meets the ball like a perfect piece of destiny
Bang!
Top corner
the ripple in the net
my team mates are all screaming
we won
11–10
I just lie there on the grass
facing up towards the sky
Mr Evans blows his whistle
and I almost start to cry
from pure joy
there's nothing in the world
as good as this
so from the bottom of the pile-on
I just smile
in pure bliss.

NEW GUY

I can see them
through the glass
thirty people
new class
can't swallow
mouth dry
deep breath
You'll be fine
feel small
hands sweat
You can do this
Don't forget
You're ready
Let's go
feet stuck
oh no
can't move
Yes you can
Get in there
Push the door
Seize the day
Hit the floor
You're amazing
You're great

Now you're here

It's fate

I'm so nervous

they look mean

I'm the worst there's ever been

That's enough

Get together

You are funny

You are clever

Let's do this

so I do

open door

stepping through

room goes quiet

people stare

try to focus on my chair

walk to board

take a pen

hand is shaking

nerves at ten

feel their eyes

burn my back

write the letters

glossy black

deep breath

turn around

'You can call me, Mr Brown.'

SNOW

Look at it.

So beautiful.

So perfect.

So pristine.

A hundred fields of perfect snow

So crisp and oh so clean.

So straight along its edges

So smooth on front and back

So many possibilities

Somebody hold me back.

The smell is so

Incredible

The colour blemish free

I want to stroke it like a cat

And make it purr for me

I'll build a world

I'll pen a song

I'll fill it with my mind

I'll pour out so much magic stuff

I'll make the pages shine

You either get it
Or you don't
So don't bother trying to moan.
This brand-new empty English book
Is mine
So get your own.

CAREERS ADVICE

What do you want to do with your life?

Asks the well-dressed woman sitting
in her comfy chair
behind her desk with the perfect rubber plant and the flat
  screen computer
with her special coffee mug from home and
photograph of her nice new family.

I'm not sure

Says the girl in loose uniform sitting
still, hands under her thighs, looking across
at the woman wondering whether this person
who seems so sure
about everything was ever ever
in her life
fourteen.

I'M SURE THERE MUST BE
ONE OF ME

WHOSE MIND IS TRULY GIFTED

WHO'S CAPABLE OF MAGIC
THOUGHTS

IMAGINATION WHIZZ KID

DOUBLE SCIENCE

As Miss Finch holds the test tube up
to show us how it's done right
I watch particles of dust float up
a tractor beam of sunlight

Each tiny speck could be a world
a microscopic GALAXY
a multiverse of possibles
from happiness to tragedy

In every world a different me
a different life to lead
which version am I living now?
And does this me succeed?

A billion different me's out there
living, breathing, ageing
how many of them sat in science
lost inside a daydream?

There is a me, right now, who's painting flames
across a ceiling
another me sits penning songs to cope
with how she's feeling

Another me was born a boy
raised by a different family
the possibles are infinite
so many me's there can be

I'm sure there must be one of me
whose mind is truly gifted
who's capable of magic thoughts
Imagination whizz kid

But I just sit and stare
at the dust trapped in the sunlight
as Miss Finch holds the test tube up
to show us how it's done right.

SOMETHING STARTS

He's younger than the others. Looks about my brother's age.

He speaks like people speak, not like he's reading from a page.

He asks you actual questions, lets you talk and not just write.

He makes you want to tell him things about your actual life.

He sometimes rushes into class, looking rough, but kind of cool.

He's the only one you can imagine living life outside of school.

He gets proper hyped when talking about characters and story.

He didn't laugh when Jacob said his favourite film was *Finding Dory*.

He seems to love his job, like he's doing what he's made for.

He makes me want to try my best to show him that I'm grateful.

He held me back yesterday when everyone was leaving.

He said he liked my work in class and asked me what I'm reading.

He didn't seem to mind when I told him I don't read.

He said he never read himself until he found the need.

He handed me a book he said he thought that I should try.

He told me I should take my time and read it by July.

He smiled and said, 'I'd love to talk about it when you're done.'

I think I'm going to try and read it later when I'm home.

REAL WORLD

Right now,
in a bunker
somewhere in the world,
there are man-made nuclear weapons with
enough destructive power to decimate
the entire planet several times over, primed and ready to be
launched at the touch
of a button by self-serving government idiots in
unfair positions of power that give them
the ability to wipe us all out in the blink of an eye

and you want me to concentrate
on Shakespeare's use of alliteration in Act Two?

ACROSS A ROOM

I know he hasn't noticed me
watching as he stares out
sitting in his bubble
he rarely speaks in class

I wonder what he hopes to be
watching as he stares out
it's like something is calling him from
outside through the glass

There's something washes over me
watching as he stares out
a feeling that we could be close
that never seems to pass

He's hypnotized me totally
watching as he stares out
I'd love to ask him what he sees
I'm just too scared to ask.

CRACKS

I see cracks
in the skin
next to my fingernail

in paving stones
and bus windows
                    my galaxy screen

In the voice that I use
with other people   and
        the space between
breaths.

I see cracks
in the ponytails
                    of girls turned away from me
in tight circles
                    around a dancing blue Bunsen burner flame.

I see cracks
in clouds
of shouted words
                        in the looks my mum gives my dad

the soles of my brother's shoes

in the faces of clocks   that don't move

I see cracks in shiny faces
under crooked headlines
            about crooked people

And no matter how these teachers
try
to cover them with paper smiles

            I know I see cracks

                        in my chances.

THOSE WHO CAN'T

You look for yourself
with every new group
you stand
in front of
you scan for that face
the one you remember
looking out from
lost
but hopeful
scared
but strong in ways
yet to blossom
telling yourself
it is your job
to water and feed them
pull back the curtains
and cover in sun
and when you find
yourself
in the midst of the others
yourself stares back
and reminds you
that all the others
are you too.

DID YOU TELL ANYONE?

NO. DID YOU?

NO.

PEOPLE ARE TALKING.

I KNOW. ARE YOU OK?

I THINK SO.

CONSTRUCTS

If caring was measured
on
a clock
would midnight be
the most
you could care
or not
caring at all?

Hey

Hey

You good?

Yeah. You?

Yeah.

Cool.

I didn't want / I'm sorry about

What? Sorry. You go.

No, it's OK. You go.

No, it's fine, seriously. My fault. What were you gonna say?

I don't know. Doesn't matter.

I wasn't sure you got my message

I did

Yeah, I figured. When I saw you, that you got it, I mean, thanks.
  For coming

It's OK.

Did you tell anyone?

No. Did you?

No.

People are talking.

I know. Are you OK?

I think so.

Good. I didn't want you to not be OK

I'm OK

You look OK, I mean, you look better than OK. Sorry

It's OK. What's wrong?

Nothing. No. I just. I.

Me too

Yeah?

Yeah

Wow

I know.

So do we say anything?

I don't know. Do you want to?

I want to if you want to. Do you want to?

I don't know

We don't have to. Not right now.

OK

OK.

HMS BIG SCHOOL

Seven years on this ship
routine
repeating
going through
motions we
grind through the days
We walk the same steps
hands in
our pockets
skirting through
trouble
searching for praise

We dream of the future
our own
independence
the freedom
to choose
what we do with our time
We're sure that we're ready
we've studied
and practised
we've sharpened

our tools
and focused our minds

Then all of a sudden
the rocks
of the real world
crunch into
the hull
tear holes in the bow
We're cast off aground
in the land
of our futures
and the only two words
we can think are
what now?

DETENTION

This will probably sound weird
to you
but
                    I love it.

It's like school but
not

It's quieter.

No shouting. No stares. No stupid giggling about nothing.

Just you   and a couple of familiar nameless faces
                    in silence
writing
an essay about why what you did   was wrong
and sitting here
thinking   in between
the lazy clock's ticks and a tired   teacher's breathing
it really feels
like

the best lesson there is.

WE SIT IN ASSEMBLY
A HALL FULL
OF STRANGERS
THE CAST OF A FILM
WHERE NOBODY'S
THE STAR

LIKE MINDS

There are crowds inside the crowds

So many people

All these people

There are shouts on top of shouts

Giant people

Scary people

There are laughs that sound like knives

Different people

Angry people

As we scurry round like mice

Little people

Tiny people

Will we ever not be scared?

Growling people

Shouty people

Will the space ever be shared?

Cliquey people

Guarded people

Where am I supposed to stand?

Confused people

Nervous people

Look for smiles that understand

Find my people

Breathe my people.

FRESH FISH

They give us a map
and our own
private journal
like they think that
we'll never
be heard from
again.
Years from now they'll find
fossils
of scattered Year 7s
buried under the feet
of Years 8
9
and 10.

We sit in assembly
a hall full
of strangers
the cast of a film
where nobody's
the star.
The ground underneath us
completely unstable
as each of us tries

to work out who
we are.

The Head beams a smile
like she's selling us something
welcomes us
into
this family
of school.
Together and separate we look
at each other
scanning for danger
searching for cool.

The bell is much louder
the building's enormous
there's so many people
it's hard to keep track.
Last year we were biggest
now we're the smallest
trying not to slip through
corridor cracks.

We're put into groups
and meet our form tutor
he's dressed like he works
in an office

or bank.
They show us how everything's
on the computer
when asked to choose passwords our minds draw
a blank.

We pay for our lunch
with a fingerprint scanner
like the food is some top secret
government plan.
We still have to queue though
same shuffling and chatter and nobody knows
what to do with their hands.

Outside we feel tiny
surrounded by giants
who just carry on like we're not even there.
It's like we're gazelles in a field full of lions
who've already eaten
so don't really care.

We meet a new teacher
who gives us a book at the end of the lesson
we're all supposed to read.
Some of us groan
as she hands us our copy

some of us hide our excitement
and leave.

Walking along
to the week's final lesson
a few of us laugh when a boy starts
to cry.
Some of us hang back to check
what's the matter
the gap stretches
into a proper divide.

We're supposed to write down
our end-of-week feelings
what we think of our first days of secondary life.
Nobody says anything very revealing
we're basically glad that we're all still alive.

Then the bell goes
and saves us
we look at the people we've chosen to sit with
just as the week ends.
We pack up the journals and maps that they gave us,
'I'll see you on Monday,'
we say to new friends.

PARTING THOUGHT

Tiny Year 7s swim
past me
like fish

Funny to think
I was ever
that small

But now
that we're leaving
I do kind of wish

I could go
back in time
and
restart it all.

ABOUT
THE AUTHOR

Steven Camden is one of the UK's most acclaimed spoken word artists. He writes for stage, page and screen, teaches storytelling and leads creative projects all over the place.

He has performed his work all around the world from Manchester to Melbourne and Kuala Lumpur to California. He moved to London for a girl, but Birmingham is where he's from.

He also has a thing for polar bears.